# Brady Brady

## and the Twirlin' Torpedo

Written by Mary Shaw

Illustrated by Chuck Temple

Stoddart
Kids

TORONTO • NEW YORK

**Visit www.templetoons.com for more Brady Brady information**

Published in Canada in 2002 by
Stoddart Kids,
a division of Stoddart Publishing Co. Limited
895 Don Mills Road, 400–2 Park Centre, Toronto, Ontario M3C 1W3

Published in the United States in 2002 by
Stoddart Kids
a division of Stoddart Publishing Co. Limited
PMB 128, 4500 Witmer Estates, Niagara Falls, New York 14305-1386

To order Stoddart Kids books please contact General Distribution Services
*In Canada* Tel. (416) 213-1919 FAX (416) 213-1917
Email cservice@genpub.com
*In the United States* Toll-free tel. 1-800-805-1083 Toll-free FAX 1-800-481-6207
Email gdsinc@genpub.com

06 05 04 03 02     2 3 4 5 6

**National Library of Canada Cataloguing in Publication Data**

Shaw, Mary, 1965–
Brady Brady and the twirlin' torpedo

ISBN 0-7737-6271-X

1. Teasing — Juvenile fiction.  2. Hockey — Juvenile fiction.
I. Temple, Chuck, 1962–  II. Title.

PS8587.H3473B738 2002     jC813'.6     C2001-902927-6
PZ7.S534258Brk 2002

*Brady and the other Icehogs support Tes when she
is ridiculed for being the only girl player on the team.*

*We acknowledge for their financial support of our
publishing program the Canada Council, the Ontario Arts
Council, and the Government of Canada through the
Book Publishing Industry Development Program (BPIDP).*

Printed and bound in Hong Kong
Book Art Inc., Toronto

**Visit the Stoddart Kids website at www.stoddartkids.com**

Brady LOVED hockey. So did his friend Tes.
When they weren't with the other Icehogs,
they were usually on Brady's backyard rink,
practicing slapshots or stuffing pucks past Hatrick.

Brady thought it was great that a
girl LOVED hockey as much as he did.

At first, some of the Icehogs wondered about having a girl on the team.
That was before the Coach got Tes to show them her "Twirlin' Torpedo".

She . . .

*leapt into the air,*
*twirled in a full circle, landed,*
*and fired the puck with all her might!*

Chester never even saw it coming. Tes had always hated her
figure skating lessons, but those spins had finally come in handy.
She was welcomed to the team, and now she was an Icehog
like the rest of them.

Today, the Icehogs were playing an *annoying* team
called the Hounds.
Brady had been up since the crack of dawn.

He liked to be first at the rink so he could high-five his
teammates as they arrived.
As usual, Tes was the next one through the door.

When everyone was there and ready to play,
the Icehogs huddled in the center of the dressing room
for their team cheer.

*"We've got the power,*
*We've got the might,*
*We've got the spirit . . .*
*Those Hounds won't bite!"*

Both teams took their positions on the ice.
The referee dropped the puck and play began.
It was then that Brady and the others heard the teasing.

"What's a *girl* doing out here? Go home to your mommy," sneered one of the Hounds.

"Did you tie your skates in a pretty bow?" hollered another.
"Why don't you go home and play with your dolls?"

Brady looked at Tes. She just continued to play.
If she heard the heckling, she was doing a great job
of ignoring it.

"Don't listen," Brady said
when he sat on the bench beside Tes.
"You're as good a player as anyone here."

"Don't worry, Brady Brady. I'm *not* going to let them get to me!"
Tes replied.
But when she went out for her next shift, the teasing continued.
And it got louder.

"Go home and bake some cookies," yelled a Hound.

"Make sure you don't break a nail!" barked his friend.

The taunts continued through the entire first period and into
the second. Brady watched Tes. She was biting her bottom lip.

As hard as she tried,
Tes could not ignore the Hounds.
She couldn't concentrate. She missed passes.
She skated in the wrong direction.
She even tripped over the blueline!

When Tes tried her "Twirlin' Torpedo",
she fanned on the puck and fell down in a heap.
The Hounds laughed even harder.

The buzzer sounded to end the second period,
and Tes was first off the ice.

In the dressing room, nobody knew what to say.
Tes looked sadly down at her skates.
"I guess I let you guys down," she whispered.

"No way! Nobody could play with all
that teasing going on!" Chester said.

"Right!" the other Icehogs chimed in.
"We'd be exactly the same, if it was us."

"Wait!" cried Brady. "That gives me a *great* idea!"

"All right, Brady Brady!"
The team huddled together to hear Brady's plan.

When the Icehogs skated out for the final period,
the Hounds just stood there with their mouths hanging open.
Some even rubbed their eyes to make sure they
weren't seeing things.

The Icehogs had a new look!
They had flipped their jerseys inside out,
tucked their hair up, and disguised their faces.

It was impossible to tell who was who!

**"Let's play hockey!"** Brady shouted, and the Icehogs flew into action.
They had never played so well — or laughed so much during a game!

The Hounds stopped teasing Tes because they couldn't tell which player she was!

*Until . . .*

. . . she lined up the puck
at the blueline,

*leapt into the air,*
*twirled in a full circle,*
*landed,*
*and fired the puck with all her might!*

Her "Twirlin' Torpedo" sailed right into the top corner of the Hounds' net, seconds before the buzzer sounded to end the game.

Tes had scored the winning goal!

The teams lined up to shake hands.
*This* time, the Hounds were first to skate off the ice
with *their* heads hanging.

"Maybe they've gone looking for a girl to help them out,"
chuckled Brady, as he high-fived Tes.

Just then, the Hounds' goalie came back onto the ice. He skated over to Tes. "Great game," he said.

"You mean, for a *girl*?" asked Tes.

"No. I mean *you* played a great game."

And a crowd of funny faces nodded in agreement.